The Mystery of
the Caramel Cat

The Mystery of the Caramel Cat

By Lynn Hall

Illustrated by Ruth Sanderson

GARRARD PUBLISHING COMPANY
CHAMPAIGN, ILLINOIS

F
HAL

Library of Congress Cataloging in Publication Data

Hall, Lynn.
 The mystery of the caramel cat.

 (A Garrard mystery book)
 SUMMARY: Willie's encounter with a feline ghost
outside a deserted mansion leads to a strange dream
about events which occurred prior to the Civil War.
 [1. Ghost stories. 2. Cats—Fiction. 3. United
States—History—1849-1877—Fiction] I. Sanderson,
Ruth. II. Title.

PZ7.H1458Myc [E] 80-22146
ISBN 0-8116-6415-5

Contents

1. A Deserted Mansion

Willie sat on the top of her tire swing and made it rock from side to side, like a bucking horse. She was getting a little too old for a tire swing, but sometimes it seemed like an old friend.

It was a beautiful Saturday in October, but Willie felt lonely. Through the lilac hedge, she could see crowds of happy, dressed-up people across the street at Annette's house.

Not that she *wanted* to spend her Saturday going to a wedding, Willie told herself. It wasn't much fun getting dressed up and staying clean. And Willie hardly knew Annette's older sister, the bride, so why should she want to go to her wedding? After listening to Annette jabber on and on about her junior bridesmaid's dress, Willie was sick of the whole wedding business.

Still, it felt sad to be alone while her best friend was wearing a long dress and white gloves, and being told how pretty she looked.

"Well I don't have to sit here and stare at them," Willie decided suddenly. She jumped down and ran the block and a half to her father's gas station. It was the nicest looking of the three stations in their little Missouri town, and Willie was proud of it.

At the side of the station was a little shed with a sign that said, "BIKE SHOP . . . Buy-Sell-Repair." Willie waved at her father, who was taking care of a customer at the pump out front. Then she went to the bike rack that held the used bikes waiting to be sold.

There were three bikes to choose from today. Willie imagined that they were a gray Arabian stallion, a small black mare, and a big bay hunter.

"I'll take you," she said to the Arabian stallion, as she wheeled the bike out of the rack. Her father approached, wiping his hands on a rag. He smiled at her in a special, tender way that he had. He always made Willie feel as though he could look into her mind and understand when she was hurt.

"Where are you off to?" he asked, still smiling.

"I don't know. Out in the country, I guess. It's a nice day."

"You bet it is, Sis. It's too nice a day to go to some dumb old wedding." He went to the candy machine and came back with a salted nut roll. "Take this, honey. Enjoy your Saturday, hear me?"

She grinned. Willie and her father understood each other.

Willie pedaled her make-believe stallion down Commerce Street, past the edge of town and out the blacktop road. She passed two gravel roads. She had already explored them on other Saturdays. They didn't go anyplace interesting.

Then she came to a third road. This road was new territory. Somehow it seemed right for today. She took it.

After about a mile of ordinary farmland, the area became hilly and more heavily wooded. Suddenly Willie slowed, and stopped.

To her left was a very narrow dirt road. Grass growing down the middle of the road made it look as though it hadn't been driven on for years. There was a sign that said "Dead-end road." For Willie, that was an invitation to explore.

Soon Willie found herself under a tunnel of trees. Pine woods closed in darkly around her. Although the road went downhill, it soon grew too rocky for Willie's bike to coast. She stopped, got off, and began to walk. "I won't go much farther," she thought. But the road went around a bend, and then another bend, and her curiosity invited her to go on.

At last both the hilly road and the woods ended at a shallow stream. The remains of a wooden bridge rose from the rocky stream bed. The posts and planks were covered with wild grapevines that gave them a ghostly look. Willie loved the place.

She looked beyond the stream bed, into an area of green-gold light. There was a meadow overgrown with lush grass, and in its center stood a big house. It was L-shaped, with pillars along the front porch. Its boards were silvered with age and neglect. Masses of growing vines covered the pillars, as though they were trying to pull them down to the ground.

Willie was already wading across the stream. She approached the house, her sneakers squishing water with every step. The house was fascinating. She saw it, not as it was now, but as

it must have been one hundred years ago. She
pictured a gleaming white mansion with sloping,
lovely lawns. Carriages would arrive, drawn by
shining horses. Women in hooped skirts would
walk beside gallant gentlemen. The house would
be full of light and life.

Imagining those people, Willie felt a pang of
sadness. They had probably never expected their

beautiful home to become the sad, sagging, dead place it was now.

"Oh, well," she thought cheerfully. "They're not around anymore, so it can be my house. I can pretend, anyway."

She tried to get to the front door, but the porch floor in front of it was rotted away. The door latch was out of reach above her head. At the side

of the house, long, narrow windows reached almost to the ground. The windows had shutters with fancy locks.

With her shirt sleeve she wiped a circle on one of the dusty windowpanes. She framed her eyes with her hands and looked in.

It was the biggest room she had ever seen. The floor was made of beautiful blocks of wood. A huge marble fireplace filled most of one wall. The room had no furniture. Faded wallpaper hung in strips from the ceiling A basket stood near the fireplace, and in the basket lay a huge, yellow cat.

A cat.

2. A Caramel-colored Cat

Willie looked again, startled. He was a huge cat the color of caramel, except for his white chin. He waved his tail in slow motion and stretched his front claws. Then, looking directly into Willie's eyes, he meowed.

The sound shattered the moody stillness. Willie jumped. She felt the hair rise on the back of her neck. Suddenly it seemed wrong to trespass and look in the windows. She sensed eyes watching her.

"That's silly," she told herself. "It's only a stray cat that moved in here. Cats do that all the time. Old, empty houses in the country are sure to have a few cats hanging around."

She backed away and moved to another window. This one looked in on what used to be a library. Empty bookshelves lined two walls. This room was smaller than the first, and square. It held a broken-legged oak table on which was stretched—

A caramel-colored cat. He looked into Willie's eyes, opened his mouth, and meowed loudly.

"It can't be the same cat," Willie thought. "He couldn't have run in here from the other room and stretched out on the table so fast. There must be two cats in there. Maybe they just look alike and have very loud voices."

The cat meowed again. He didn't seem to be asking for help or crying in pain. He just seemed to be talking to Willie, as cats sometimes do when they live close to people.

17

Willie left the library window and continued on around the house. There were no more low windows on this side. At the back of the house she stopped and tried the back door. It was locked. Then she walked along a path away from the house to several small sheds. One had been a woodshed. Inside there were still bits of wood and bark on the dirt floor. Another had been a laundry shed. Its door was partly open. Willie pushed it in and looked inside. The room held a huge brick fireplace, a clutter of wooden washtubs, and a workbench along one wall.

The cat was stretched out on the workbench. His slitted eyes looked directly into Willie's. He seemed to be waiting for her.

He rose, stretched his back into a high arch, and came toward Willie.

"Meow," he said in his loud voice.

For a moment, they stood looking at one another. Then Willie turned and ran down the sunny, sloping meadow of lawn. She splashed

through the stream and went squishing up the hill to her bike. The cat did not follow.

She rode home, excited. Now that she was safely away, she wasn't sure why she ran. She loved cats and had never been afraid of them. But this was no ordinary cat. There was something strange about the way he appeared and reappeared, the way he looked at her and seemed to be trying to say something to her.

"I just hope I can make Annette believe me when I tell her," Willie thought.

It was almost dark by the time Willie got home. Many cars were still parked around Annette's house. Lights shone through open doors and windows, and Willie heard loud voices. But now the wedding wasn't important to Willie. She had other things on her mind.

That cat—

Her mind was so full of the puzzle of the cat that she almost walked past Mr. Hill without seeing him.

20

He was sitting on his front step, next door to Willie's house. "Aren't you speaking to me anymore, Miss Jefferson?" he called.

"Oh, hi. I didn't see you sitting there." She went across the yard toward him and sat on the bottom step. It would be several hours yet before her father closed the gas station and came home for supper. In the meantime, Mr. Hill was good company.

He nodded toward Annette's house. "You didn't go to the wedding?"

"No. Who wants to get all dressed up on Saturday? I went for a bike ride instead. I found a neat old mansion, far out in the country."

"Oh?" Mr. Hill sounded interested. "Where was that?"

"About three miles out on the blacktop road, and then that way." She waved her arm.

"I know the place you mean. It was called Meadow-something, as I recall. It was quite a place in its day."

Willie sat up. "You know about it? Tell me." Mr. Hill was a retired schoolteacher, and he was full of interesting information.

He shrugged. "I don't know much. It was supposed to have been a house on the underground railroad. That's about all I remember hearing about the place."

"Underground railroad?" Willie frowned. "I didn't see any tracks."

Mr. Hill laughed. "Not that kind of railroad, Willie. The underground railroad was a system to help runaway slaves get north, where they would be free. People hid the slaves in houses all the way to Canada. The houses were owned by people who wanted to help the slaves, and each house had some sort of hiding place. Some had a hidden room, or a cave, or just a small space under a floor, with a secret door."

Willie's eyes opened wide.

"If a runaway slave could get to one of these houses," Mr. Hill went on, "he could hide there safely and be fed. When it was safe to move on, the owner of that house would help him get to the next house along the way. Finally, the slave would get far enough north so he could come out of hiding and not be returned to his owner."

Willie grinned. "It sounds exciting."

"It was a very dangerous business for the slaves and for the people who helped them," Mr. Hill said soberly. "Anyone caught helping a runaway slave was punished by the law or even killed."

"And that house I found this afternoon was one of those railroad places?"

"That's what I've heard."

Willie thought about this information silently. It was interesting, but it didn't shed any light on the question that was still in her mind.

Finally, she said, "Mr. Hill, something funny happened out there. I was looking in the windows of that house. In the first room I saw a cat lying in a basket and looking out at me. It was a big yellow cat with a white chin. When I looked in the next room, there was the same cat again. Then I went to a shed at the back of the house, and that same cat was in there, too."

"Hmm. Couldn't it have been more than one cat? Two or three yellow stray cats around an empty house wouldn't be unusual."

Willie shook her head. "It was the same cat. I know it."

"Well, then, he must have been following you from room to room."

She shook her head again, but she couldn't come up with a good answer. She just felt sure there was something funny about the way that cat appeared so often.

3. Does the Cat Belong?

Just then Annette came across the street toward them. Her long dress and white gloves gleamed in the dusk.

"How do I look?" Annette asked, holding out her skirt and twirling.

"You look just like a princess, honey," Mr. Hill said.

Annette smiled, then looked at Willie. "It's a pretty dress," Willie said, trying to sound as though she meant it.

The two girls went to Willie's house. "You want some supper?" Willie asked.

"No, thanks. I've been eating all afternoon. You should have seen the wedding cake, Willie."

While Annette chattered on, Willie made herself a sandwich and took it to her room. Annette followed.

"And we all had our pictures taken," Annette said. "I was in three of them. A photographer from the newspaper was there, so my picture might be in the paper. And my cousins from Florida—"

Willie settled on her bed and appeared to be interested in what her friend was saying. But she heard nothing, for her mind was full of runaway slaves and underground railroad houses. She pictured the mansion as she'd seen it today, and then tried to add the people, like actors on a stage. She thought of the slaves, fleeing for their lives and their freedom. She thought of the brave man who owned the house, risking everything in order to help strangers. And the cat. *No. The cat didn't belong in the picture.* Willie shook her head.

Annette stopped dancing around the room and sat on the foot of the bed. Carefully, she smoothed her skirt over her knees. "You're not saying very much," Annette said in an accusing tone.

"Well, I had a kind of exciting day, too. You haven't asked me what I did."

"What did you do?" Annette's tone clearly said that nothing could be as exciting as a wedding.

Willie said, "I went for a long bike ride out in the country. I found an old deserted mansion that used to be part of the underground railroad. It has a ghost cat in it."

Willie was startled at what she'd said. "Where could that idea have come from?"she wondered. She hadn't been thinking of the cat as a ghost. That was silly.

"That's silly," Annette said. "You're just making that up because you're jealous." She laughed. To Willie, the laugh sounded stupid.

."I'm not making it up," Willie said. "Ask Mr. Hill. He was just telling me about the underground railroad."

"Oh, Willie." Annette waved a white-gloved hand. "How could trains run underground? They'd have to dig tunnels everywhere, and why would they do that?"

Willie rolled her eyes toward the ceiling but didn't answer. She was beginning to wonder why Annette was her best friend. It seemed as though the older she and Annette got, the farther apart they became.

"What about the ghost cat?" Annette prodded.

Willie just shook her head. "Forget about it. I was just kidding."

Annette stood up. "I'd better get on home. I just wanted to show you my dress. See you tomorrow."

"Yeah."

She followed Annette out of her room. Then Willie went to the kitchen, where she turned on the stove and started to fix her father's supper. It was almost nine, and he'd be starved when he got home.

Her father came in a few minutes later, gave her a hug, and sat down at the table.

"Did you have a good time this afternoon?" he asked as she put food on a plate.

"Yeah, pretty good."

Willie wanted to tell him about the house and the cat, but Annette's reaction to the story made her decide to wait. She wandered back to her room and closed the door.

She was glad that Annette had gone. It was not a nice way to feel about your best friend, Willie admitted to herself. But for now, that was the way she felt. She needed to be alone, to think about the house and the cat. She couldn't get the cat out of her mind.

Willie got ready for bed. She ran out to the living room to give her father a good-night hug. Then she jumped into her bed and wiggled down under the sheet until she was settled. It had been four years since her mother had left, and often Willie went all day without thinking of her. But bedtime always brought back happy memories. Now there was only one parent to hug.

Outside her window, the wind blew and spatters of rain hit the screen. In a minute it was raining hard. Willie got up and lowered the window, leaving it open just a few inches. She enjoyed the sound and smell of the rain.

Finally, she drifted off to sleep. Some time later the bed bounced lightly, as though something had landed on one corner and was still there. Willie didn't want to wake up.

4. Pieces of a Dream Puzzle

The something moved toward her. It stepped onto Willie's stomach and settled there, purring.

"I'm having a dream," Willie thought. "I'm dreaming that the caramel cat is here in my bedroom—on my bed. But he couldn't be. There are screens on all the windows. My door is closed. A cat couldn't have gotten in, so I have to be dreaming. I won't move or open my eyes, and the dream will disappear."

The purring stopped, but the weight remained on her stomach.

"It's not real. I'm asleep. I'm dreaming."

The caramel cat tucked his paws neatly under his chest and stared at Willie. He narrowed his eyes until they were green slits.

Slowly, Willie's body relaxed, and she slept soundly. A dream came—

It was like no dream Willie had ever had. It was vividly clear.

Willie dreamed that she was a cat, the same caramel-colored cat she had seen that afternoon. It seemed strange, and yet somehow natural, to be just inches from the floor, looking up at everything. She could look along her nose and see whiskers sprouting from her face. She could twitch her tail and feel it sweep the floor behind her.

She was in a small room, smaller than her bedroom. The room was dark, but Willie could see outlines and shades of color. It seemed to be a cellar room. The walls were of rough stones, painted white. A dirt floor was under her paws. The ceiling was made of rough timbers, and there were no windows. On the far wall, slivers of light showed through a plank door from the room beyond.

Two women were in the room with her. One was young; the other woman was much older.

The older woman was small and bent. Both had dark skin. They wore long skirts of rough cotton, and their clothes looked as though they had been worn for days. Their faces showed the strain of constant fear.

The old woman spoke. "We're not going to make it. We're at the end now. They're going to catch us and take us back."

"Hush, Annie. We're going to be fine." The young woman's voice was soft and kind, but weary. It was as though she had spoken these words many times before.

"You might survive all of this, Charity," the old woman said. "You're young. You can stand more than I can, and you've got more reason to keep on trying."

Charity's face softened. "Yes. I've got a reason . . . my husband, already escaped and free, is waiting for me in Canada. It's the best reason a woman can have for going on."

"But most runaway slaves are caught. You

know that. If they catch us, they'll kill me. I'm old and useless. But they'll do worse to you. We shouldn't have tried it."

"Shush." The young woman's voice was crisp. "Some of us are caught, but lots of us get away. Edward made it. He got to Canada and got his freedom. He managed to send word back to me, so I'd come, too. If he can do it, we can. We've got friends to help us, Annie. We've got all these good people from Mississippi to Canada, who have been taking us into their homes and hiding us. Think of the risks they're taking, just to give us a chance to be free."

Willie made a noise and moved closer to Charity.

Annie looked down at Willie and said harshly, "That cat is going to be the end of us, Charity. He's going to make a noise at the wrong time, and we'll be caught. I just know it. You were crazy to bring him."

Charity reached down and stroked Willie's

neck. "I couldn't leave him behind. He's the only creature on this earth who ever loved me, except Edward."

Annie snorted. "That's foolish. Cats can always take care of themselves. He'd have gotten along fine if you had left him. Now you've put us both in danger, bringing that noisy animal along."

Charity opened her mouth to argue, but sud-

denly both women froze. They huddled close together, so still they seemed not to breathe.

From beyond the blank door they heard voices.

"I'm sorry, Mr. Evans." A man was speaking. "We've got our duty to do. We hear that you've been a part of the underground railroad, hiding runaway slaves in your house and helping them get away to the north. We've got a notice that two women slaves are in this area. They might even be here. There's a big reward for the young one. We've got to check it out."

"Now, John, you've known me for almost fifteen years. We've been neighbors and fellow Grange members. You ought to know I wouldn't be involved in the underground railroad."

The voices came closer. They were just beyond the wall.

"We have to search your house, Evans. It's our duty. I'm sure you understand."

Willie heard a pounding on the wall. She moved closer to Charity. Charity's hand reached down and held Willie tightly. It was too tight. Willie felt panic and struggled to get away. She opened her mouth and cried.

Sudden silence came from the room beyond.

"I heard a cat," a voice said. "Men, get in here, quick. I heard a cat somewhere behind that wall."

The old woman whimpered.

Mr. Evans's voice came through to Willie. It

was firm but with a note of fear in it. "That was just one of the outside cats. You can hear them from in here. That's all it was, gentlemen. You have my word."

"Stand aside, Evans, and don't try to leave. You might as well tell us where they're hiding. It'll go better for you if you cooperate."

Mr. Evans's voice rose. "I'm telling you—"

"Jack! Tom! Come here and help me move this."

Willie heard something very heavy being dragged across a floor. Something made of glass fell and broke. There was a light, clattering sound, like dishes being moved. Terror pressed Willie close to Charity's leg.

5. Captured

Sudden light burst into the room. Men came and seized the two women. Annie cried out, but Charity was silent.

"Get along here, you two." The man holding Charity jerked her roughly.

One of the men turned to Mr. Evans. "You're under arrest for concealing and aiding runaway slaves," he said.

The door slammed, and once again the room

was dark. Willie heard Charity wail, "My cat, I've got to get my cat. I can't leave him."

Willie crouched and trembled. She didn't understand what was happening. But she knew that she had caused something dreadful to happen.

She had cried out at the wrong time.

She flung herself at the door. It was open just a crack. She squeezed through. The house was empty. Outside, horses had been mounted and were now being ridden away into the night.

Willie woke so quickly her arms and legs jerked. She was wet with sweat. Her pajamas clung to her, and the sheet wrapped itself around her. Her pillow was on the floor.

She sat up and turned on the light. Her hands trembled, and her breath came unevenly, but she forced herself to be calm. She took long, slow breaths, smoothed the sheet carefully over her legs, and put her pillow back in place.

"There now," she told herself. "I'm okay. It was just a dream. But what a strange dream! It was so real. So clear. I was right there. And I was—was I? I dreamed I was a cat. And before that, I thought there was a cat in my bedroom. Was that part of the dream?"

She turned off the light and lay back, but her mind was running at full speed. Everything was tied in together—the old house in the country, the caramel-colored cat, and the dream.

But what did it all mean?

During breakfast the next morning, and all through Sunday School and church, Willie was haunted by her dream. As soon as she could get out of the house after dinner, she took a bike from the rack in her father's shop and pedaled out of town toward the dead-end road.

"I have to see that house again," she thought as she rode. "And the cat. That dream was so real, I can't believe it was just something I made up. If I can get into the house and see if there really is a hidden room like the one in my dream—if I can find it—"

Her imagination went no further than that. She wasn't sure what she was trying to prove. She knew only that the house, the cat, and her dream were somehow connected. She had to try to find out what she could.

She left her bike at the stream and waded across. The sky was a brilliant blue broken by heavy gray clouds left from last night's storm. The clouds blew across the sky behind the house. Willic shivered.

After she reached the house, she went from window to window, trying them all, hoping to find something unlocked. The doors she could reach were all locked too. Only the front door and the windows on the front porch were out of her reach, for the porch floor had rotted away.

"Darn," she muttered after jumping several times, trying to reach the knobs on the broad, carved double doors. She went around the house again, looking for an unlocked door or window. She came back to the front of the house and stood staring at the double front doors. From where she stood, it looked as though the lock had rusted and was hanging loose.

"If I could just get up there," she thought.

The outer framework of the porch was still solid. Broad steps led up to the rim of the porch. Willie looked among the boards on the ground within the shell of the porch. Finally she found one that looked long and strong enough to hold her weight. With some effort, she managed to get it into position so it made a bridge from the steps to the door.

Quickly, she stepped across it, holding her breath. When she tried the door, it creaked open. She stepped inside, expecting to see the cat. He wasn't there.

Willie looked around. She was in a broad entrance hall. Ahead, a fancy stairway went up to the second floor. Doors opened from the first floor entrance hall into broad, bare rooms. Quickly Willie looked through each of the rooms. She went up the stairway and walked through the bedrooms on the second floor. Then she went up to the smaller bedrooms and store-rooms on the third floor.

The house had many large rooms that once had been beautiful. But Willie knew they weren't right. They didn't fit her dream. She came back to the entrance hall and sat on the steps.

"The room in my dream was more . . . like a cave. Something underground, like a cellar. That's it!" She got up and began opening doors. A door beneath the big staircase proved to be the cellar entrance. The steps leading down were dimly lit by sunlight from the cellar windows.

Cautiously, Willie felt her way down into the cellar. Once there, she straightened and breathed more easily. She was in a large room. From the center rose a massive brick chimney, twelve feet wide. It held a huge open fireplace and two smaller openings covered by heavy iron doors. Baking ovens, Willie guessed.

From the books she had read, Willie knew that southern mansions often had summer kitchens away from the main part of the house. Heat from the ovens would not add unwelcome heat to the main house. The room she stood in now appeared to have been a summer kitchen, or perhaps a servants' kitchen. Beside the fireplace was a long, scarred wooden table. Massive low sinks lined one wall. There was even an oval braided rug on the floor, but it was so dusty and faded it had no color at all.

Slowly Willie walked around the room. There were doors to smaller rooms on either side. One had once been a coal storage bin. One room held rows of empty wine racks. Others were piled with junk—bits of rope, gunny sacks, and rusted tools.

As she explored, Willie kept in mind the size and shape of the house above her. The basement rooms seemed to fill that size and shape exactly. There was no space that might hold a hidden room.

"This whole thing is probably silly," she thought. But she returned to the summer kitchen and stood thinking. She didn't want to give up yet.

She frowned and tried to remember the details of the dream. The room in the dream had no windows. Only a very little light came through the tiny cracks in the plank door. She remembered a dirt floor.

Then she remembered something else. At the moment when the slaves were discovered, there had been the sound of something heavy being shifted ... and another sound. What had it been?

Dishes! It sounded like dishes breaking, or something similar. Willie's excitement rose. She looked around for a piece of furniture that might have hidden a door.

There was nothing except a crude corner cupboard which still held a few cups and plates.

She ran to it. The cupboard was narrow and

high, about two feet deep along its sides and almost ceiling high. The bottom part was an enclosed cupboard, but the upper part had open shelves. The back of the cupboard was made of planks.

Willie's heart beat rapidly. Maybe, maybe—

6. The Secret Room

She stepped closer for a better look and felt a ridge through the soles of her sneakers. She dropped to her knees and felt a groove scraped in the floor. It curved out from one corner of the china cupboard, as though the cupboard often had been swung out and away from its corner.

She gripped the cupboard and pulled. It shifted, but only a little. She braced one foot against the wall and put all her strength into the effort.

The cupboard came away from the wall, inches at a time.

At last Willie could squeeze behind it. A small doorway led into . . .

. . . *the room in her dream.*

From within the room, the caramel cat rose and meowed his welcome.

As he stepped toward her, Willie froze. The cat stared up into her eyes. It was as though he were trying as hard as he could to tell her something. A great sadness burned in his eyes.

"What is it?" If her question was foolish, Willie didn't notice. She just wanted to talk to the cat, to somehow ease the pain he seemed to be feeling.

He opened his mouth as if to meow, but no sound came out.

"Come here, come, kitty." Willie knelt and held out her hand to him. He crouched and lashed the air with his tail, but came no closer to her.

"I'm your friend. I want to help you. What's the matter?"

He looked at her again, and his eyes seemed to plead for understanding.

Finding the room and seeing the cat again did not satisfy Willie. The room and the cat did not answer the important questions. They only proved that her dream had a basis in reality. She had to find out more. She had to know if the cat she'd seen was a real cat with an uncanny ability to get into unexpected rooms, or whether he was a ghost cat.

She could not believe in ghost animals. And yet, the more she tried to find an answer, the more she felt that there was only one logical answer.

The cat she saw must be the ghost of the cat who was brought to this house by runaway slaves. It must be the cat whose meow caused his mistress to be captured. If her imagination could stretch to accept that fact, was it also possible that the cat haunted the house out of some sense of guilt? Had he come to Willie's bedroom and, in some way, put his memory of the capture into Willie's mind? Had she felt the cat's fear at the time of the capture in her dream?

No. It was fantastic. Impossible.

But was it really entirely impossible? Wasn't television also impossible to imagine before it had been invented? Weren't dreams that warned of coming disasters impossible? Yet they happened. Willie often sat, fascinated, while her father talked about things like that with Mr. Hill from next door.

After a few days of thinking about little else, Willie decided to tell her father about the cat and the dream. She waited until he was settled for the evening on the front steps. Then she told him everything about the deserted house, the cat, and the dream. She finished by telling him about finding the hidden room.

"I pulled back the cupboard and looked in.

There was the room, just like I dreamed it. And the cat was there, too."

Her father thought for a minute. Then he asked, "What did you do?"

"I talked to him, but I didn't try to touch him."

Her father was silent for so long, Willie had to prod him. "Well? What do you think?"

Mr. Hill came out of his house just then, waved, and went toward his lawn mower.

Willie's father called, "Ralph, come here a minute. Willie's had an interesting experience. See what you think about it."

Mr. Hill listened while Willie told him about her dream and her discovery of the room.

"Sounds to me like that was more than just an ordinary dream," he said. "I believe that dreams can be messages from people who have died, or maybe from some source of knowledge that we don't yet understand."

"I don't get it," Willie said flatly.

"It is pretty confusing," Mr. Hill admitted.

Willie frowned and finally said, "Do you mean the dream I had was some sort of a message the cat was sending me? Like a phone call or something?"

Mr. Hill said, "Or like a movie being projected from the cat's memory into yours. I'm just guessing. It might not have been that at all. It might have been just your imagination."

They were silent, all three following thoughts of their own. At length Mr. Hill said, "There is something you might do, if you want. You might try finding out more about the house. Read about its history and the people who lived there. Maybe you'll learn something that will tell you if all this is just your imagination, or whether you've had some sort of extrasensory experience."

"What does that mean?"

Mr. Hill shrugged. " 'Extrasensory?' That means things that happen in ways we can't explain, because we don't yet know enough about how the human brain works. Things like mind reading, or dreams that foretell something that will happen in the future."

"Oh."

"Why not check the library?" he went on. "They have some good books on local history. I'm pretty sure there's one on underground railroad houses in this part of the country."

Willie's excitement grew. "I'll go! I'll go check it out tomorrow morning. I could skip school for something as important as this, couldn't I, Daddy?"

"Absolutely not."

She sighed. "Okay. After school, then."

7. A Forgiven Cat

The school day passed slowly. When the last bell finally rang, Willie shot out the door like a stone from a slingshot.

"Hey, wait up," Annette called.

"Can't. I'm going to the library. Talk to you later."

Annette stared after her.

Willie walked by the children's room in the library, where she usually went to find new horse books. Today she went to the main desk and asked for a book on underground railroad houses in Missouri.

The librarian smiled as she went back through the shelves. "You must be writing a paper for school."

"No, I'm just interested."

"Well, this should be what you're looking for."

Somewhat to Willie's surprise, the book was not thick or old. It was a large, thin book. She took it to the oak table in the reading room and settled down to read.

On each right-hand page was a sketch of a house in brown ink. On the facing page were a few paragraphs telling a little about the house's history. Willie turned each page with hope and a feeling that was close to fear.

She had almost reached the end of the book, when there it was ... her house. "Meadowbrook, south of Leadtown, Missouri, built in 1791."

Quickly Willie read the less interesting parts of the Evanses' family history. Then she slowed and began reading in earnest.

"During a period of almost seven years, just before the outbreak of the Civil War, Meadowbrook was used as a hiding place for slaves seeking their freedom in the north. The hiding chamber was believed to have been a room built underground, leading from the cellar under the main house.

"Mr. Joseph Evans was the owner of the house at this time. He was said to have been sympathetic to the Negro cause because of his own childhood experiences. He was an orphan and was raised by an elderly aunt, who often locked young Joseph in a clothes closet. She was thought to be crazy by those who knew her.

"Joseph Evans helped more than two hundred slaves to their freedom. One day he was caught, tried, and convicted. He was sent to prison, where he took his life.

"Mr. Evans was famed for the purebred horses and dogs which he bred at Meadowbrook. Sadly, it was his love for animals which led to his undoing. Two women slaves came to him for protection in their flight from their owner in Mississippi. They had with them a pet cat who, according to local legend, meowed when officials were searching the house."

Stunned, Willie wandered out of the library.

The caramel cat had been real, she thought. He had lived more than one hundred years ago. The cat, and Charity and Annie and the men outside the plank door . . . all had once been in the house. Her dream was not just a dream, but a memory that was carried through the years. And that memory had been projected, through the caramel cat, into Willie's mind.

Why? She strained to understand. Then she thought, "Maybe he just needed to be forgiven."

Suddenly, Willie wanted to see that cat. "It's silly," she told herself. "How can I forgive him, or make him feel better? It wasn't *me* he harmed; it was Charity and Annie. But—"

She turned around and looked at the clock over the door of the bank. It was after four—late to be starting out on a long bike ride. But her mind was made up. She ran all the way to the gas station and pulled a bike from the rack. Her father was busy with a customer, so he didn't notice when she left.

The ride to Meadowbrook seemed longer than before, but finally Willie was standing in the broad entrance hall of the old house. She started to call, "Here, kitty, kitty," but it just didn't sound right. The name wasn't right for calling a ghost cat. Instead, she began walking through the broad, bare rooms of the mansion. Even though she walked as quietly as she could, her footsteps echoed through the empty rooms.

She found the cat where she had first seen him. He was in the huge, sunny parlor at the end of the house. He lay in the basket beside the mar-

ble fireplace. To Willie it seemed as though he waited for her.

Quietly, she went up to him. When she was close to the fireplace, she folded her legs and sat, Indian-fashion, on the dusty floor.

"I know who you are now," she said softly. The cat stared and blinked.

"That is, I think I know." She smiled as the cat watched her. Then she went on, "This whole thing is pretty weird, you'll have to admit. Here I am, sitting in an old house and talking to a cat that lived a hundred years ago. I still don't believe this, but it must be true."

The cat moved his tail. He seemed to be listening.

"If you really are—were—Charity's cat, then you must be staying around here, haunting this house, because you feel so sad about what you did. Is that it?"

He blinked and stared at Willie's face.

"I don't know what happened to Charity, old

cat. But she must have loved you a lot. And she must have been a really nice person. I bet she forgave you a long time ago. I bet she understood that you meowed because you were so scared. You didn't mean to give away the hiding place. I bet she still loves you just as much as she ever did, wherever she is now. Don't you think so? Don't you think she forgives you?"

For an instant, the cat continued to stare at Willie, as though he understood her words. Then, slowly, he seemed to relax. His eyes closed, and the silent old room was filled with the sound of purring.

How do people
LIVE ?

Macdonald

In prehistoric times, people used to live in caves, or in rough shelters made of animal skins. Over the ages they learned to make stronger shelters and homes for themselves.

In hot countries people still made tents from animal skins, or they built huts made from palm leaves or mud. In cold countries they made houses of stone. Where there were forests, people could make houses from wood.

Nowadays many of us live in buildings made of brick or concrete. But all over the world there are other kinds of homes. Would you like to live in one of them?

This house is built from bundles of rushes and woven straw. It stands on an island made out of mud and rushes, in the marshes of Iraq.

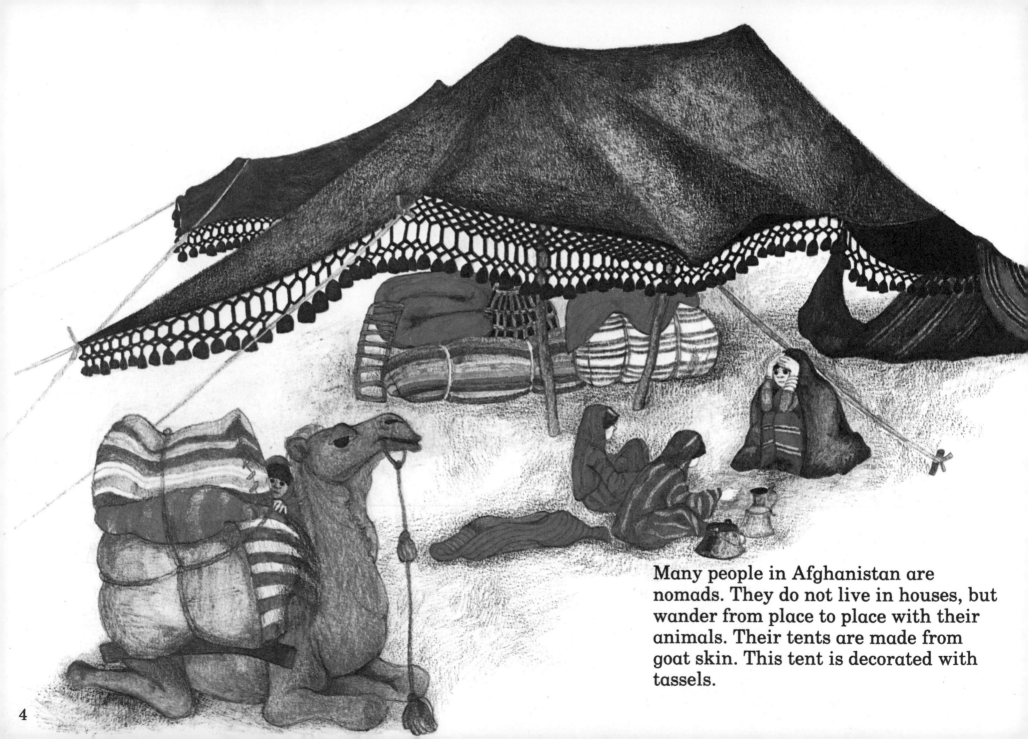

Many people in Afghanistan are nomads. They do not live in houses, but wander from place to place with their animals. Their tents are made from goat skin. This tent is decorated with tassels.

4

One valley in Turkey is famous for its cave houses. Hundred of years ago, people carved holes in the rock to make homes, stables and store rooms. The caves are warm and cosy. Only birds can reach the front door without a ladder!

5

This log cabin is in the mountains of Siberia, in the Soviet Union. It is built from birch trees. There are no windows, but a hole in the roof lets out the smoke from the fire.

6

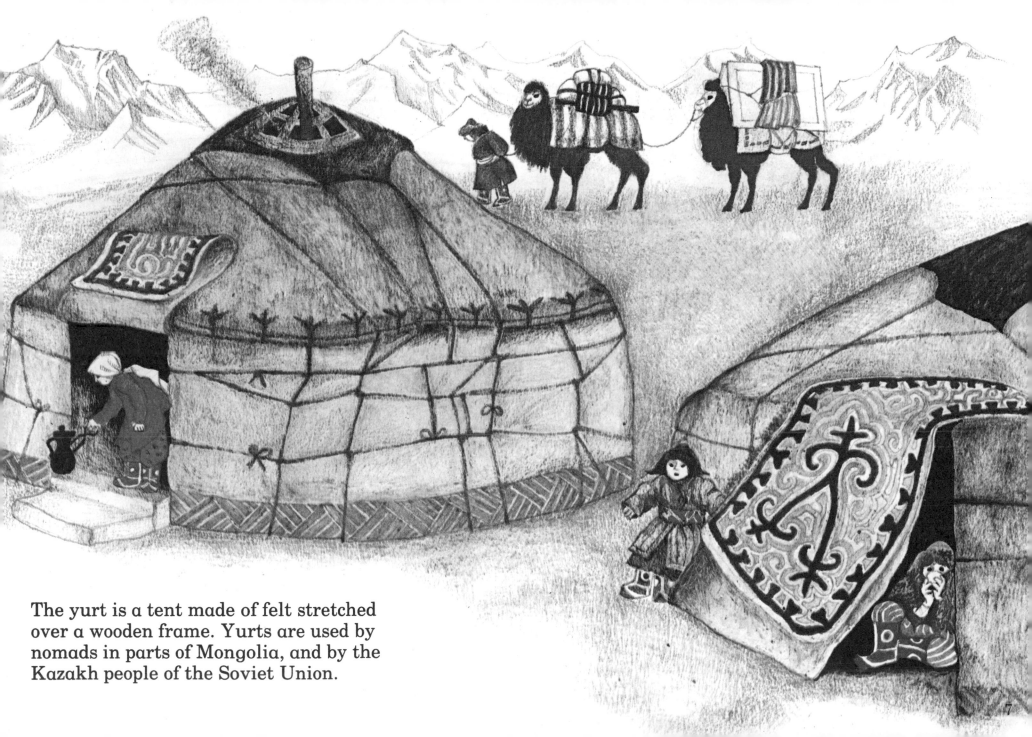

The yurt is a tent made of felt stretched over a wooden frame. Yurts are used by nomads in parts of Mongolia, and by the Kazakh people of the Soviet Union.

In Rajasthan, in northern India, some families still travel from place to place in a covered ox-cart. They are craft workers, and they use the cart as a workshop as well as a home.

8

These beautiful houses are built on tall stilts. They are to be found on the island of Sulawesi, in Indonesia. They have carved wooden steps and decorated doorways.

9

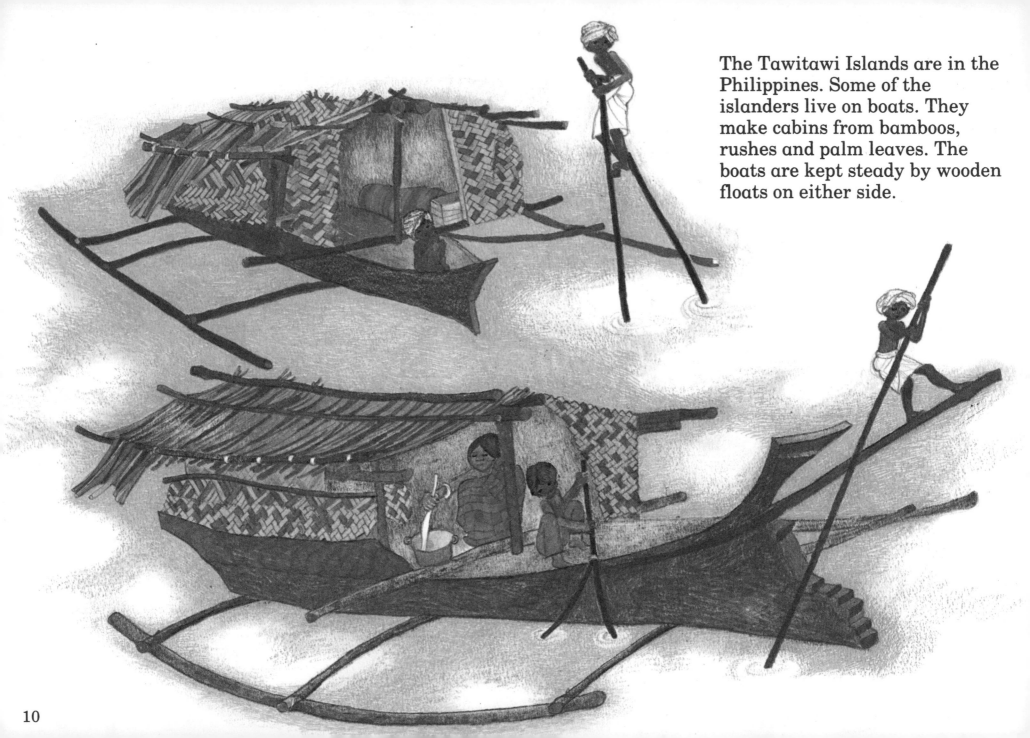

The Tawitawi Islands are in the Philippines. Some of the islanders live on boats. They make cabins from bamboos, rushes and palm leaves. The boats are kept steady by wooden floats on either side.

These wooden buildings in New Guinea are used for storing vegetables. The people themselves live in smaller, airy buildings, like the one on the far left of the picture.

11

In Papua-New Guinea there are stilt houses with high roofs. They are made of wood and carved with faces and strange patterns!

12

Have you ever played in a tree house? On the island of Mindanao, in the Philippines, some people live in tree houses. To reach the treetops you must climb up tall ladders made of wood.

Old Japanese houses were made of wood. The roofs were tiled or thatched, and the windows made of paper.

14

In harbours in China there are
thousands of houseboats. The big ones
are called junks, and the little ones are
sampans.

Outside the homes of the Tlingit
Indians, in northwest America,
stand rows of carved totem
poles. They show animals and
faces from old Indian stories.
The bear is real enough, though!

16

The Inuit, or Eskimo, people of the Arctic used to live in tents during the summer. In the winter they lived in round houses built out of stone or blocks of frozen snow. These were called igloos.

17

The Blackfoot Indians of the American plains used to live in tepees. These were tents made of buffalo skins stretched over long wooden poles.

18

The Indians of Brazil cut down trees to make a clearing in the rain forest. Here they build huts made of branches. The roof of palm leaves keeps out the tropical rain. They sleep in a hammock tied between two branches.

The Tuareg people are nomads. They cross the hot Sahara desert with their camels, sheep and goats. They use the animals' skins to make large, cool tents.

Houses like this may be seen in Nigeria and in Mali in West Africa. They are built of mud and the walls are often decorated with patterns. Inside there is a courtyard.

The buildings around Lake Chad in West Africa are made of wood and mud. Some of the buildings have special holes at the top. These ones are for storing grain.

22

On the plains of Africa there are all kinds of wild animal. There are herds of cattle too. The families who look after them camp in little huts. They make the huts from branches and cover them with cow hide.

23

The Nubian desert is in Sudan.
It is one of the driest places
in the world. The houses there
are made from bricks of mud,
and covered with patterns and
pictures.

The Dogon people live
in Mali, West Africa.
Some of their villages are
built on rocky hillsides.
Grain is stored in these
thatched huts, which
stand on wooden
platforms.

The Aborigines of Australia used to walk from place to place in search of food and water. Where they stopped, they built shelters made of sticks and grasses.

A MACDONALD BOOK
Illustrations © Erika Urai 1979
English text © Macdonald & Co (Publishers) Ltd 1985
First published in Hungary by Corvina Kiadó, Budapest

English text by Philip Steele
Based on the Hungarian original by Lajos Boglár

First published in Great Britain in 1985
by Macdonald & Co (Publishers) Ltd
London and Sydney
A BPCC plc company

Reprinted 1986
All rights reserved
ISBN 0 356 11158 X

Printed and bound in Hungary

Macdonald & Co (Publishers) Ltd
3rd Floor
Greater London House
Hampstead Road
London NW1 7QX